This book belongs to:

who was made
BEAUTIFULLY,
PERFECTLY &
LOVELY
in every way!

This book is dedicated to every girl who has ever doubted her beauty, her strength & her courageous spirit! Release her!

To the three Maries (Holly, Tonja, Sonia), Babs (Ms. Shapiro) & all my loving friends & family who reminded me never to give up!

Doubleday and the colophon are registered trademarks of Penguin Random House LLC.
HAPPY HAIR is a registered trademark of Happy Hair.

Visit us on the Web! rhcbooks.com

Educators and librarians, for a variety of teaching tools, visit us at RHTeachersLibrarians.com

Library of Congress Cataloging-in-Publication Data
Name: Roe, Mechal Renee, author, illustrator.
Title: Happy hair / written & illustrated by Mechal Renee Roe.
Description: New York : Doubleday Books for Young Readers, [2019] |
"Originally self-published in slightly different form in 2014."
Summary: "A visual and rhyming celebration of African-American girls' hair" —Provided by publisher.
Identifiers: LCCN 2018046100 (print) | LCCN 2018051434 (ebook)
ISBN 978-1-9848-9554-7 (hc) | ISBN 978-1-9848-9555-4 (glb) | ISBN 978-1-9848-9556-1 (ebk)
Subjects: | CYAC: Stories in rhyme. | Hair—Fiction. | Hairstyles—Fiction. |
African Americans—Fiction. | Self-esteem—Fiction.
Classification: LCC PZ8.3.R6185 (ebook) |
LCC PZ8.3.R6185 Hap 2019 (print) | DDC [E]—dc23

MANUFACTURED IN CHINA
10 9 8 7 6 5 4 3 2 1

Random House Children's Books supports the
First Amendment and celebrates the right to read.

HAPPY HAIR®

Written & illustrated by MECHAL RENEE ROE

Doubleday Books for Young Readers

I LOVE ME

FULL 'FRO, CUTE BOW!

i love being me!

SMART GIRL, COOL CURLS!

i love being me!

CUTE CROP, DON'T STOP!

i love being me!

PRIMPED 'N' PRESSED, DRESSED TO IMPRESS!

i love being me!

♥

SO MUCH HAIR, EVERYWHERE!

i love being me!

FRESH DO, TOO COOL!

i love being me!

TOWER HIGH, REACH THE SKY!

i love being me!

COOL VIBES, ACCESSORIZE!

i love being me!

LOVED
& FREE!

i love being me!

♥

POM-POM PUFFS, PRETTY & STUFF!

i love being me!

♥

BRAIDS TIGHT, DONE RIGHT!

i love being me!

LOVED LOCS, PRETTY FROCKS!

i love being me!

YOU ARE MADE BEAUTIFUL

HAPPY HAIR®